MILES IS THE BOSS OF HIS BODY

Written by:
Samantha Kurtzman-Counter
& Abbie Schiller

Based on the screenplay by:
Abbie Schiller & Christine Ecklund

Illustration:
Valentina Ventimiglia

Book design:
Deborah Keaton

THE MOTHER COMPANY

TODAY WAS A SPECIAL DAY: IT WAS MILES'S 6TH BIRTHDAY!
HE BOUNCED UP THE FRONT STEPS AFTER SCHOOL,
EXCITED TO CELEBRATE WITH HIS FAMILY.

HEARING THE SCUFFLE, MOM ENTERED THE KITCHEN WITH LITTLE MAX.
"BOYS: STOP ROUGHHOUSING! PIZZA SHOULD BE HERE ANY MINUTE..."

MILES HAD BEEN WAITING ALL DAY FOR HIS FAVORITE DOUBLE-MEATY-PEPPERONI-SAUSAGE-PINEAPPLE-HOLD-THE-ONIONS-EXTRA-CHEESY BIRTHDAY PIZZA!

AS MILES STARTED RUNNING TO THE DOOR, MAX GRABBED HIS SHIRT!

"MAX, LET GO!"

MILES DIDN'T QUITE KNOW WHAT TO SAY. A BIRTHDAY CHICKEN WAS DEFINITELY...DIFFERENT!
"UH... THANKS... BIRTHDAY CHICKEN."

THE PIZZA GUY REACHED OUT TO PAT MILES ON THE HEAD.
"HAPPY BIRTHDAY, LITTLE RIPPER!"
MILES COULDN'T TAKE IT ANYMORE...

MILES STORMED INSIDE TO TALK TO HIS FAMILY. HE'D HAD ENOUGH!

"EXCUSE ME, PLEASE! I HAVE SOMETHING I WANT TO SAY: IT'S MY BIRTHDAY, AND I'M TIRED OF BEING PINCHED, NOOGIED, HUGGED TOO TIGHT, PICKED UP, GRABBED, TICKLED, AND TOUCHED IN WAYS THAT I DON'T LIKE. I'M SIX YEARS OLD AND I'M THE BOSS OF MY BODY!"

MILES STOMPED ANGRILY OFF TO HIS BEDROOM AND SHUT THE DOOR.

"BUT WHAT IF I DON'T WANT TO HUG OR KISS SOMEONE? CAN I JUST WAVE OR GIVE A HANDSHAKE TO BE POLITE INSTEAD?"
"YOU CAN DECIDE WHAT FEELS RIGHT, BUDDY."
"SOUNDS LIKE A PLAN."

THE WHOLE FAMILY GATHERED AROUND THE BIRTHDAY CAKE TO CELEBRATE. PROUD TO BE **THE BOSS OF HIS BODY**, MILES STOOD TALL AND FELT SO HAPPY TO KNOW THAT HIS FAMILY LOVED AND RESPECTED HIM. HE COULDN'T IMAGINE A GREATER BIRTHDAY GIFT IN THE WHOLE WIDE WORLD.

"HAPPY BIRTHDAY MILES!"

THE END.

A NOTE TO PARENTS AND TEACHERS

It can be very difficult to talk to young children about personal safety. How can we best communicate which kind of touch is unsafe without scaring our kids or introducing them to concepts we're not comfortable with? Given the atrocities against children that we hear about every day, how can we empower our kids to keep themselves safe from harm — especially when we're not around?

It is our goal at The Mother Company to offer young children effective tools and engage them in these potentially lifesaving conversations. Guided by the curriculum of renowned child safety expert Pattie Fitzgerald of Safely Ever After, Inc., we've found that one great way to broach the difficult topic of safe body boundaries is by teaching kids the phrase "I'm the Boss of My Body." This important concept empowers children to stand up to any kind of touch that feels wrong and trust their instincts to keep themselves safe.

In *Miles is the Boss of His Body*, we check back in with our old friend Miles (the main character of our bestselling *When Miles Got Mad*) as he spends the majority of his sixth birthday fending off his well-meaning family, who just won't stop tickling, pinching, and giving him birthday noogies! The big revelation here is that Miles realizes he does have a choice - he summons his courage and proclaims, "I am six years old and I'm the boss of my body!" The outcome? Miles's family couldn't be more proud of him. Given the unfortunate truth that roughly 90% of the harm done to children is not by a stranger, but by someone they know, Miles's story can inspire in young children the confidence to take charge of their own bodies in any situation.

It is our aim to create fun, beautiful, engaging stories for children that tackle some of life's most important social and emotional issues. We hope kids will enjoy, relate, and laugh alongside Miles as they absorb essential tools, language, and tips to keep themselves safe throughout life.

– *Abbie Schiller & Sam Kurtzman-Counter, The Mother Company Mamas*

With the goal to "Help Parents Raise Good People," The Mother Company offers award-winning children's books, videos, apps, activity kits, events, parenting resources, and more. Join us at TheMotherCo.com.

THE MOTHER COMPANY